For Paul
(who took me back to school)
and to all the children and teachers,
past and present, who have made
my times at Langley School so special,
with warmest love

And also to Plymbridge Woods nearby

First U.S. edition 1993
Published in Great Britain in 1993 by Walker Books Ltd., London.

Library of Congress Cataloging-in-Publication Data is available.

ISBN 1-56402-219-6

10 9 8 7 6 5 4 3 2 1

Printed in Hong Kong

The pictures in this book were done in
pen and ink and watercolor.

Candlewick Press
2067 Massachusetts Avenue
Cambridge, Massachusetts 02140

The WILD WOODS

SIMON JAMES

CANDLEWICK PRESS
CAMBRIDGE, MASSACHUSETTS

Jess was walking with her grandad
when they saw a squirrel.
"I'd like to take him home,"
Jess said.

"You can't keep a squirrel,"
called Grandad.
"They're too wild."

"I'll take care of him," Jess said.
"But you can't keep a squirrel,"
called Grandad. "What are
you going to feed him?"

"He likes our sandwiches,"
Jess said.

"You can't keep a squirrel,"
shouted Grandad.
"Where's he going to sleep?"

"I'll make him a bed in
my room," Jess said.

"Hurry up, Grandad. I think
I found a waterfall."

"You can't really keep a
    squirrel," Grandad whispered.
"I know," said Jess.
"He belongs in the wild."

"I like being in the wild,"
Jess said. "Can we come
back tomorrow?"
"Well . . . okay," said Grandad.
"Good," Jess said, "because . . . "

"one of those
ducks might need
taking care of."